THE CREEPER DIARIES

BOOK TEN

GET A JOB, CREEP

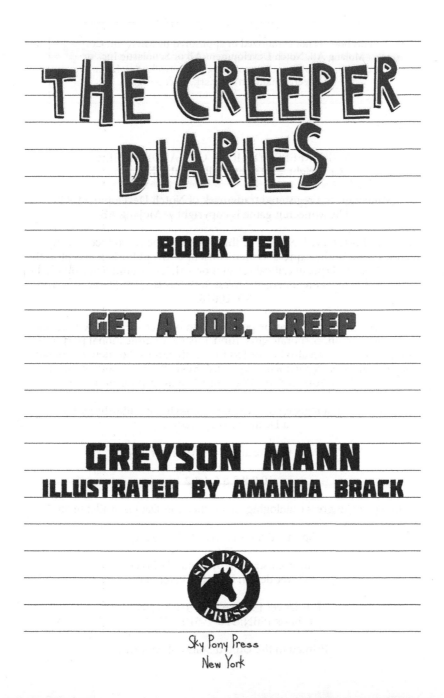

THE CREEPER DIARIES

BOOK TEN

GET A JOB, CREEP

GREYSON MANN
ILLUSTRATED BY AMANDA BRACK

Sky Pony Press
New York

Visit our website at www.skyponypress.com.

10 9 8 7 6 5 4 3 2 1

Library of Congress Cataloging-in-Publication Data is available on file.

Special thanks to Erin L. Falligant.

Cover illustration by Amanda Brack
Cover design by Brian Peterson

Hardcover ISBN: 978-1-5107-4104-1
E-book ISBN: 978-1-5107-4124-9

Printed in the United States of America

DAY 1: SATURDAY

No more pencils,
No more enchanted books,
No more of Mrs. Enderwoman's
DIRTY looks!

Summer's here! YAAAASSSSSSS!!!!!

Tonight was my FIRST night of freedom, and I spent it with my good buddy Sam Slime. I thought we'd do something FUN, like jumping on his trampoline or writing rap songs or playing my new videogame. It's called HUMANCRAFT, and it's all about building villages for humans and then sending creepers and zombies into the villages to see how many humans you can freak out. (Good times.)

So you can imagine my surprise when Sam said he wanted to go look at KITTENS. Um . . . WHAT now?

I reminded Sam that creepers and kittens don't exactly get along. Well, creepers and CATS don't get along—no matter how much Sam wants me to be BFFs with his cat, Moo.

But Sam said this new Critters Unlimited store opened up at the Mob Mall, and he REALLY wanted to go see the kittens.

When I heard about the store, I figured I should go with Sam—not to check out the kittens, but to see if the store sold any squids, like my pet squid Sticky. I've been thinking about getting him a buddy.

So I went with Sam to Critters Unlimited, and they DID have squid! I ditched Sam by the kittens, and then I walked past the rabbits (meh), the spiders (gross), and the silverfish and endermite farms. (SERIOUSLY??? Mobs PAY for that kind of thing?)

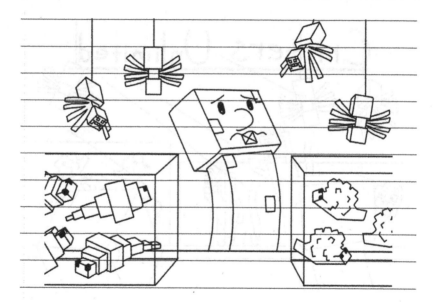

Before I could even get to the squid, I spotted something else:

PARROTS.

I've been on a parrot kick ever since I saw one in
Kid Z's newest video. Kid Z is my favorite rapper,
and he actually taught his PARROT how to rap too.
It's true—I wouldn't lie about that kind of thing! The
bird sits on Kid Z's shoulder and repeats anything
that comes out of Kid Z's mouth. ANYTHING. It even
DANCES! The rapping parrot video got a gazillion
likes online. It probably broke some kind of record.

5

So as soon as I saw *the parrots* at Critters Unlimited, I KNEW I had to have one. I mean, if Kid Z's rapping parrot can go viral, why can't mine?

I picked out one that looked exactly like Kid Z's—a big red bird with a black beak and yellow and blue patches on its wings and tail. THAT was the bird for me, I was sure of it. I mean, until I checked the price tag.

400 EMERALDS? REALLY??? You could buy a used MINECART for that price!

So I walked down _the aisle past_ all the red, green, and grey birds until I found _the_ SMALLEST parrot—a tiny turquoise guy with a _patch_ of green above his beak and a bright yellow belly. That bird was selling for 150 emeralds, which seemed like a real bargain, let me tell you.

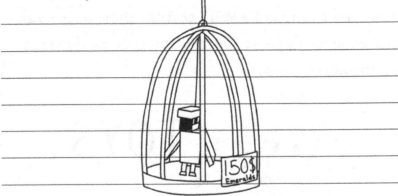

At least that's what I told my dad when I got home.

A real bargain, Dad. You can't pass up a deal like this—they're practically GIVING that bird away!

Dad barely looked up from the book he was reading. "Better start saving your allowance then," was all he said.

But Dad KNOWS I'm not a save-your-emeralds kind of creeper. Emeralds are like hot potatoes. Give me a few, and I can hardly WAIT to toss them back over the counter down at the toy store or candy store or fireworks store.

I had a better idea: "How about an advance on my allowance?" I get 10 emeralds a week. So I figured I'd only need an advance for 15 weeks, which is about how long summer lasts. "And I'll never ask for an advance again," I threw in there, just to sweeten the deal for Dad.

He set down his book. He not only set it down, but he closed it, without even marking his spot—which was NOT a good sign.

"Gerald," said Dad, "emeralds don't grow on trees." Then he said a bunch of other stuff, like "Nobody gets anything for free" and "You have to work for what you want, because then you'll appreciate it more." But all I heard was BLAH, BIDDY, BLAH, BLAH, BLAH.

It was pretty obvious that Dad was giving me a big fat NO.

Then he REALLY took things too far. "Gerald," he said, "I think it's time for you to get a JOB."

WHOA. Where'd THAT come from? I blame it on my big sister, Cate. She's gone all summer lifeguarding at some beach with coral reefs and swimming turtles. (Between you and me, she packed a LOT of bathing suits, so I think she's in it for the boys. But WHATEVER.)

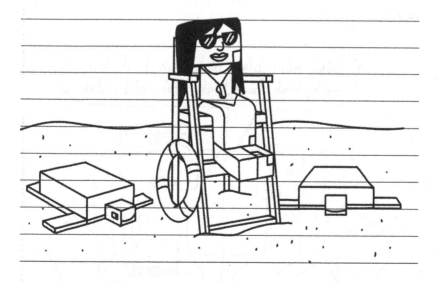

I knew the "get a job" conversation was going nowhere good, so I tried creeping out of the room. I mean, a creeper has to know when to cut his losses and run. But Mom blocked the doorway. "A job?" she said. "What a great idea!" (I really hate it when grown-ups gang up on me like that.)

Dad practically jumped out of his chair and said, "How about yardwork? You could mow our lawn. You could mow the NEIGHBOR's lawn!"

GREAT idea, Dad.

I'm pretty sure I've never even set foot on the neighbor's lawn. Why? Because that's trespassing, and I'm a law-abiding creeper.

Also, our neighbor has a mean old ocelot that I call Sir Coughs-a-Lot. And that cat and I made a deal a long time ago that he'd stay on his side of the fence, and I'd stay on mine. So I will NOT be going over there to mow the lawn any time soon.

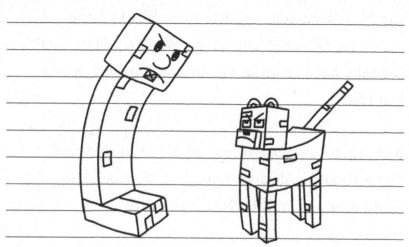

Then Mom jumped on Dad's minecart and threw out a few lousy ideas too. "You could help out at the farm, Gerald—you know, where you learned to ride a pig. I hear they've got llamas now!"

Well, I couldn't believe Mom was bringing THAT place up again. First of all, I did NOT learn to ride a pig. I mean, I tried. But let's just say that pig-riding didn't really work out for me.

Second, I like llamas about as much as I like pigs.
And Mom KNOWS that, because we all had to ride
llamas last summer when our minecart broke down in
the middle of the desert. (But that's a whole other
story.)

"Yeah, I think I'll take a pass on that one," I told Mom.

I figured Dad would back me up, because he likes
llamas even less than I do. But all he said was, "Why?

Give us ONE good reason why you shouldn't mow lawns or do farmwork to earn those emeralds, Gerald."

That's when I started to sweat. I really didn't appreciate being put on the spot like that. But then it hit me. I couldn't do those jobs because they would make me SWEAT. And sweating makes me itchy. And I ALREADY have really itchy skin.

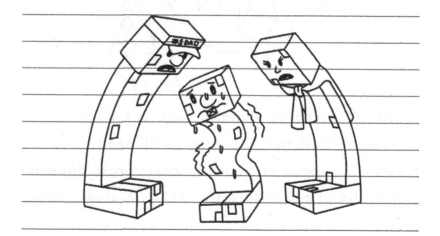

So I told Dad that. I was pretty proud of myself for thinking on my feet, let me tell you.

But Dad just said, "A little sweat never hurt a creeper. When I was your age, son, I had to work in the MINES all summer, blowing up tunnels. I sweat bucket-loads, and then I had to carry those buckets all the way out of the mine at the end of each day."

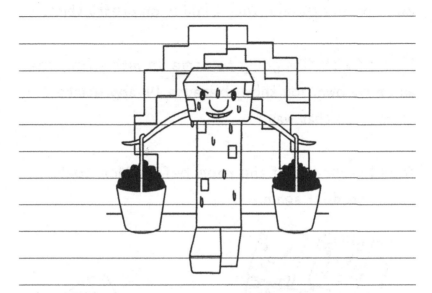

HA! Good story, Dad. I wanted to laugh out loud, but then he'd probably launch into another story about how he had to walk ten miles across the Taiga to get to school every night. And then walk through hot lava in the Nether just to get home again each morning. Why do grown-ups have to be so DRAMATIC???

Anyway, I knew I had to put a stop to that conversation before things got REALLY out of hand.

So I told Dad I thought getting a job was a GREAT idea, and that I wished I'd thought of it myself, and that it would really teach me a lot about the value of an emerald. Yup, I laid it on pretty thick.

I closed with "I'm going to come up with a few ideas all on my own. You know, because I'll appreciate them more that way."

Then I crept out of the room before Mom could block the door again.

Genius, right?

So now I'm back in my room, ready to make a plan for how to get that parrot. I think it looks something like this:

30-Day Plan for Getting a Rapping Parrot

- Get a job that does NOT involve pigs, llamas, hard labor, or sweating.
- Earn ~~150 emeralds~~ 110 emeralds (because I'll get 40 emeralds for allowance this month)
- Buy my parrot down at Critters Unlimited.
- ~~Teach that bird to rap, just~~ like Kid Z's!

But why stop there? Here's one more:

- Make a video of my rapping parrot, sit back, and WATCH it go viral.

Yup, I'm going to come up with my own genius money-making idea. But I'll come up with it all on my own, Dad—thank you very much.

DAY 3: MONDAY

Okay, well I didn't think up the perfect job ALL on my own. I mean, it wouldn't be fair to leave my good buddy Sam out of this money-making opportunity, right?

So as soon as I woke up last night, I went over to his house. I found him jumping on the trampoline with Ziggy Zombie, which was kind of a letdown. I mean, if Sam and I came up with a get-rich-quick idea, we'd probably have to split the money THREE ways now. Bummer.

Anyway, I got right to the point. "Sam!" I said, "I bet you're saving money for one of those kittens you saw at Critters Unlimited, right?"

I was surprised when he shook his jiggly head no. "I'm saving for a tablet," he reminded me.

Oh, CRUD. I'd almost forgotten that Sam's tablet was broken. And I'd really tried to forget the fact that I was the one who broke it during our field trip to the Taiga. Let's just say that a creeper should NOT try to video his run down a frozen waterfall using a tablet he borrowed from his best friend.

When it happened, I promised Sam that I would chip in on a new tablet for him. I didn't really think that one through—I mean, I would have said pretty much anything just to make him stop blubbering.

But now I wished I could eat those words. I mean, how am I supposed to help Sam buy a tablet AND save for a parrot at the same time?

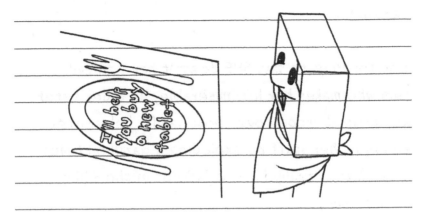

So I changed the subject. "How'd you like to find a genius way to make some money?" I asked.

Ziggy stopped jumping, wiped the drool off his chin, and said, "I'm making money this summer by baby-zombie-sitting."

HUH. That was an idea I hadn't thought of. I mean, I watch my baby sister, Cammy, all the time, but

I've never gotten even a single emerald for it. I asked Mom about paying me once, but she was like, "Spending time with your siblings is not WORK, Gerald."

Easy for Mom to say. SHE doesn't have an Evil Twin who makes her life miserable, an older sister who gets all mopey over boys, and a baby sister who ruins her stuff by exploding a gazillion times a day. Yup, I really hit the jackpot in the sibling department.

But Ziggy's baby sister, Zoe, is actually _pretty cool._ We've had some good times together, making up nursery raps and stuff.

"How much do your parents pay for baby-zombie-sitting?" I asked, all cool and casual like. "I could probably help out with that."

Then Sam had to ruin the moment by asking me to help babysit HIS baby brothers too. And that's NEVER going to happen. Why, you ask? Because those mini slimes are gross and snotty and oozing stuff ALL the time. Mr. and Mrs. Slime couldn't pay me enough to hang out with the triplets, let me tell you.

"OR . . . " I said, thinking fast, "maybe we could do some CRITTER-sitting." I figured if I brought up critters, Sam would start talking about Moo and would totally forget about babysitting.

Except that plan backfired too. Because right away Sam asked me to watch Moo while he's at camp next month. And then Ziggy asked if I could watch his pet SPIDER when he goes on a family minecart trip in August. GREAT.

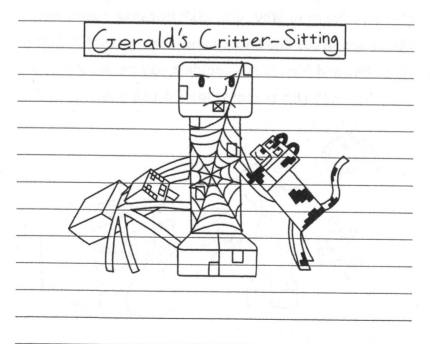

Gerald's Critter-Sitting

"Um, I think I have to keep my schedule open in case Eddy Enderman needs help walking his wolf," I said.

It wasn't my best comeback. I mean, I want to walk a wolf about as much as I want to spider-sit. But I had to say SOMETHING.

Luckily, Ziggy Zombie had just come up with a NOT-so-genius idea of his own. "We could sell stuff at the market!" he said. "Like humans do."

Ziggy's kind of obsessed with human villages. He likes to wander in and scare the humans every chance he gets. It's a zombie thing, I guess.

But I pointed out a couple of problems with Ziggy's plan. First of all, I reminded him, mobs aren't ALLOWED at the market. I mean, humans would just run away screaming—and take their emeralds with them. Second, the market is open during the daytime, and Ziggy can't be outside in the daytime. (I guess he gets a sunburn or something.) "But other than THOSE teeny-tiny little problems," I said, "it was a REALLY good idea, Zigs." Sometimes you have to throw a zombie a bone.

After that, we were fresh out of ideas. And it was looking like I wouldn't be buying a parrot any time soon.

Then I got home this morning, and EVERYTHING turned around—thanks to Mom.

See, I guess all my talk about earning emeralds inspired Mom to get a job. Yup, she signed up yesterday to be a rep for Restore Your Health Incorporated. It's this company that sells vitamins, minerals, and other healthy stuff. But it's not an actual store. Mom gets to sell the stuff right out of our house!

She opened up a box and showed me some of her products:

- Dried kelp and seagrass, which are full of something called "antioxidants." (I didn't ask Mom what that meant, because I was afraid she would make me eat some of that green powder straight up. GROSS.)

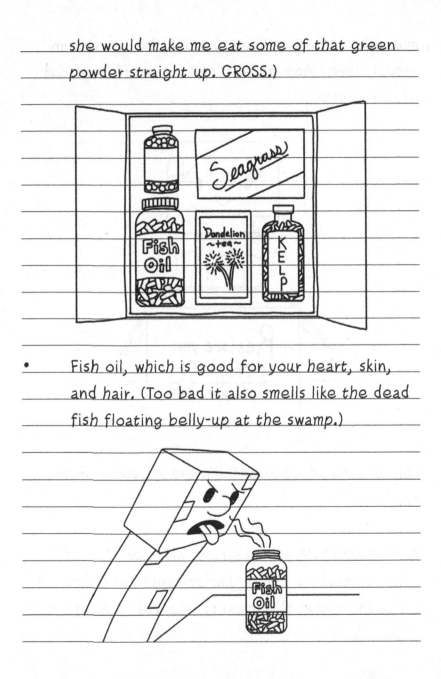

- Fish oil, which is good for your heart, skin, and hair. (Too bad it also smells like the dead fish floating belly-up at the swamp.)

- Dandelion tea: Those bright yellow flakes are supposed to help with upset stomachs and gas, Mom says. (Remind me to pocket some of that for Sam. The slime is VERY gassy.)

After she put her products away, Mom got all up in my face and said, "Gerald, you TOO could be the next rep for Restore Your Health Incorporated."

Say WHAT?

When I told Mom I was probably too young, she laughed and said she was just practicing her sales pitch. I guess if she can convince two more friends to become reps by the end of the month, Mom gets 20 PERCENT of their sales.

Well, I'm pretty good at math. So I know that 20 percent of 100 emeralds is 20 emeralds. And that 20 percent of 1000 emeralds is 200 emeralds. Mom could earn 200 emeralds for doing practically NOTHING—just for working with a couple of friends. Talk about a genius way to make money!

So now I'm wondering how I can get a piece of that action. Can I sign up my OWN friends for some kind of sales gig? And take a cut?

I may not be big on yardwork or farming or babysitting or catsitting, but I AM big on ideas. I mean, I'm the ideas guy. It's about time I started earning emeralds for those ideas, right?

So now I've got some thinking to do. And some friends to go see tonight, as soon as I get up.

That parrot is pretty much in the bag—er, on my shoulder. I can hear the rapping already . . .

Listen up, bird,
Cause you're in luck.
I'll take you home
And RAP you up.

Teach you rhythm
So we can groove.
Whaddya say, bird?
It's your move!

DAY 4: TUESDAY

So Mom's still looking for mobs to join Restore Your Health Incorporated. I might have to give her a few pointers, because last night, I signed up TWO employees with Gerald Creeper Jr. Incorporated. Yup. Pretty proud of that.

I mean, Sam wasn't totally on board at first. I had to sweeten the deal by saying I'd chip in on his new tablet. (You know, since I was the one who put the chip—er, crack—in it in the first place.)

And Ziggy turned me down because he's going to be busy babysitting this summer. So Sam wanted to invite his girlfriend, Willow Witch, to join our business. I guess she wants to earn money for a new cauldron or something.

Well, right from the start, I had a BAD feeling about inviting Willow. See, hanging out with Sam and Willow is like being the third wheel on a rusty old minecart. Willow wants to go one way. I want to go the other way. And Sam almost ALWAYS follows his girlfriend, leaving his good buddy Gerald to crash and burn. Been there and done that, thank you very much.

Plus, Willow asks a LOT of questions. When we found her down at the swamp, she was all like, "Wait a sec,

Gerald, why do we pay YOU 20 percent of what we earn?"

I almost said, "Because I'm the BRAINS of the operation. Genius ideas don't come cheap, you know."

But Willow doesn't appreciate me talking about my genius. So instead, I said the 20 percent would go toward "marketing and advertising." I don't even know where I got those words—they just came to me. Brilliant, right?

WRONG.

"Do you know anything about marketing and advertising?" Willow asked, cocking her head.

"Sure!" I boasted. "I was a reporter for the Mob Middle School Observer. I've got some SERIOUS writing skills."

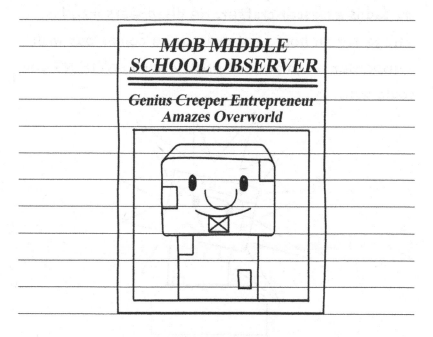

"Yeah, but writing isn't really marketing or advertising," she pointed out.

That was when I came up with another genius idea. (Like I told you, I'm the ideas guy.) "Well," I said, "did I mention that your 20 percent will ALSO go toward our selling stand? My dad is going to help me build it this week—the super deluxe model. And you'll have your OWN special spot at the counter."

Well, that did the trick. Every mob knows that my dad is a master crafter. He disappears into his garage for an hour, and presto—he comes out with a dispenser or an anvil or pretty much ANYTHING you could want.

36

I knew I'd hooked Willow with the whole "super-deluxe selling stand" thing, because her nose started twitching. "So what will we sell?" she asked.

"Hot chocolate!" said Sam. The slime LOVES hot chocolate with whipped cream, the kind we get down at the Creeper Café.

But I had to shoot that idea down. (That's what they pay me the big bucks for.) "Sam," I said, "doesn't whipped cream give you gas?"

"Well, yeah."

"And doesn't caffeine make you super jiggly?"

"I guess."

"And won't it be like 90 degrees outside this summer?"

"Probably."

"So do you think selling hot chocolate at a stand all summer is a great idea?"

Sam shook his head—and melted into a green pool of disappointment. I felt bad for the guy, but someone's gotta look out for him and steer him in the right direction.

That was when my Evil Twin, Chloe, crept into the swamp with her friend Cora Creeper. Turns out, they were looking for Sam.

"You got any more of that totally awesome homemade slime?" Chloe asked Sam in her I'm-being-sweet-because-I-want-something voice.

For some reason, Chloe and Cora are really into slime lately. Chloe has been trying to make it at home, but Mom put the kibosh on that. Maybe it was because the sticky, gloppy stuff got EVERYWHERE. It stuck on the floor and all over Cammy and all over her baby dolls and even in Sock the Sheep's wool. (Yes, we have a pet sheep named Sock. Don't even get me started on that one . . .)

So now Chloe tries to get her slime from Sam, who happens to have mounds of slime balls at home.

Before Sam could answer, Willow spoke up. "Sam is SELLING his slime now," she said. "Five emeralds a batch."

That was *pretty* genius, I gotta say. And Chloe looked really surprised. I was afraid she was going to blow sky-high when Willow asked her for money, because my Evil Twin is FAMOUS for her blow-ups.

But she didn't. Instead she whispered something to Cora, and then she said, "Sure, okay. I'll be back after I get my allowance."

"Wait, you're going to pay FIVE emeralds for a hunk of SLIME?" I blurted out. I mean, I didn't want to get in the way of a sale for Sam, but I couldn't believe Chloe fell for Willow's sales pitch—just like that.

"Sam makes the best slime," Cora explained with a shrug. "It's SUPER stretchy and doesn't stick to anything."

HUH. Go figure. So Sam had his first sales idea, thanks to Willow—and my Evil Twin. And right after

that, Willow said she was going to brew up some
potions to sell at our stand.

I hadn't really thought that far ahead. But I didn't
want Sam and Willow to know that the big-ideas guy
didn't have any ideas. So I said the first thing that
came to mind: "Rap songs, of course." I said I'd
make up a rap song for any customer who came to
the stand, kind of like how artists draw pictures of
mobs at fairs and stuff.

Willow looked like she was going to ask a whole lot
of questions about that, but I cut her right off. I
told her I had to get home to make that stand with

Dad. In fact, I promised my friends we'd have our stand up and running by SATURDAY. See, I happen to know that lots of mobs get their allowance on Fridays. So by Saturday, they'll be DYING to spend those emeralds!

Now I'm waiting for Dad to get home from work, and I'm crossing my toes, hoping he'll help me build the stand. If he DOESN'T, I'll be forced to build one myself. And that might NOT be one of my genius ideas, because I'm a way better rapper than I am a crafter. Just sayin'.

Wish me luck.

DAY 7: FRIDAY

Dad said YES to helping me build the stand. Woo-
hoo!!! I almost kissed the old guy.

That's why I haven't written in my journal for a
couple of nights—I've been busy. Dad wanted
to get going on the stand right away, probably
because he was tired of Mom practicing her sales
pitch on him with all that dried kelp and seagrass
stuff.

He even seemed kind of proud of me for coming up
with the sales-stand idea. "Gerald," he said, "you're
showing some real INITIATIVE."

That's one of his favorite words. I think it means I did something without him harassing me about it, like taking the trash to the lava pit without being asked.

So we had that stand built by this morning, and it's a sight for sore eyes, let me tell you. It's wide enough for me and my friends to fit in—even Sam, who's kind of a wide dude. And the counter comes all the way up to my chest, which means there's lots of room to store stuff down below. And there's space at the top of the stand where we can hang some of our "marketing and advertising" (a.k.a. a SIGN). Genius!

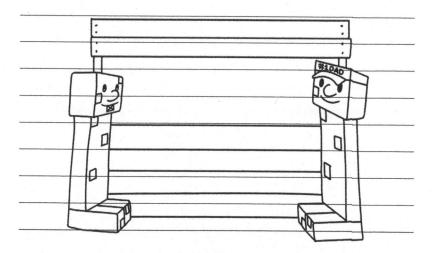

Tomorrow night, Sam, Willow, and I are going to wheel this thing to the big field behind Mob Middle School. That way, all the poor saps who are just getting out of summer school Saturday morning will pass our stand on the way home.

Forget going to the Mob Mall this weekend, kids. There's a NEW shop in town: Gerald Creeper Jr. Incorporated. Get your ice-cold potions here!

DAY 8: SATURDAY

Well, I learned a lot today. Sales are a ROCKY road.

At least the road we took to get our wooden stand to the schoolyard was rocky. And hilly. And LONG.

We had the stand strapped to an old minecart, and Willow, Sam, and I push-pulled it to school. Actually, Willow was lugging a bunch of potions too, so she wasn't much help. And Sam had flung his bag of slime balls on top of the stand, which added a LOT of extra weight. So by the time we got to school, I was sweating buckets. I might as well have been working down in the mines with Dad.

But then Willow set up all her potions on our counter, and I'm not gonna lie—those colored glass bottles were kind of pretty in the moonlight. Sam stuck his sign to the top of the stand, advertising his homemade slime. And I got my pencil ready to do some rapping. I couldn't wait to actually earn EMERALDS for my mad rap skills!

When the bell rang, we all got ready for the crowds that we knew would come our way.

But the only "crowd" turned out to be Chloe and Cora. Chloe wanted to see what kind of slime Sam was selling. SHEESH. How many emeralds did my Evil Twin have in her piggy bank? Was Dad giving her a bigger allowance than me?

I tried to keep it together. I mean, Chloe WAS a customer after all. And when Sam said he'd brought some especially stretchy slime, Chloe was all over that. She bought two batches—probably just in case Cammy got a hold of one of them. And Cora bought one too.

So chalk three sales up for Sam and his slime. I tried to get Chloe and Cora to buy rap songs too, but Chloe was all like, "I get plenty of those at home, thanks."

Then Ziggy came by with his baby sister, Zoe, along with some dark-skinned zombie with straw-colored hair. "This is my cousin Husky," said Ziggy. "He's visiting from the desert."

Well, normally I'd be all over a mob from the desert, because Husky probably knows my idol Kid Z, who lives in Sandstone. But "Husky" rhymes with all sorts of things, so instead of asking him about Kid Z, I made up a rap right there on the spot.

"Five emeralds, and I'll write you another one,"
I said to Husky. But he just kind of grunted
something. (Zombies aren't really known for their
conversational skills.)

Zoe Zombie usually LOVES my raps. But this morning,
she was all about buying a slime ball. After Ziggy paid
for that, he said he was fresh out of emeralds. He
even turned his pockets inside out to show me. Yup,
nothing but a bunch of crusty crumbs in there. GROSS.

Then Whisper Witch showed up from out of nowhere
to see what kinds of potions Willow was selling. I
tried my sales pitch again.

I threw in some dance moves for free, but Whisper just stared at me.

Then she bought a potion of invisibility from Willow and was gone in a flash.

"Gerald, don't scare off the customers," Willow said, as if MY rap was what made Whisper run away. But everyone knows the girl is super shy. So I really didn't appreciate Willow's suggestion.

What DID I appreciate? Taking 20 percent of her emeralds at the end of the morning. Yeah, that felt pretty good. Because even though my rap songs weren't bestsellers, my idea for the stand WORKED.

I'm back home counting my emeralds as we speak.

Mom says it's a good idea to keep a log of sales. She showed me her "log," which is really just a book with a lot of empty pages. (Mom's sales this month haven't been stellar.)

I'm a journal kind of guy, so I figure it can't hurt to take down a few notes, right? Here goes:

Now I'm not gonna lie—it kind of hurts that Sam's slime went all gangbusters and my rap songs didn't. But getting 18 emeralds kind of softened that blow.

I put the emeralds in my piggy bank right away. Now I'm trying to sleep, but my eyes are WIDE open.

Sticky is having trouble sleeping, too. He's just floating in his aquarium, staring at me. Maybe he can tell our lives are about to change. That I'm going to strike it rich with Gerald Creeper Jr. Incorporated. That any day now, I'm going to bring home a parrot that RAPs. And then our videos will

go viral, reaching every mob and squid in the whole
entire Overworld.

"Brace yourself, buddy," I said to Sticky. "It's going
to be a wild ride."

DAY 10: MONDAY

Last night, Mom wanted to have a family night. She said I couldn't go set up my stand, that no one was going to work. But when I caught her on the phone with Cora Creeper's mom, trying to recruit her to be a salesperson for Restore Your Health Incorporated, I busted her.

"You're WORKING, Mom!" I said.

And she was all like, "Oh, fine. Go work your stand for a little while, Gerald. But be home for an early breakfast—roasted porkchops and crispy potatoes."

Mom sure knows how to get to me. She burns her chops to a crisp, just the way I like them. So I told Sam and Willow we had to make short work of our sales.

We set up our stand down at the swamp, where lots of mobs go to hang out. Within half an hour, Willow's potion of night vision had sold right out. I think even Sam was jealous of her sales, until he busted out his glow-in-the-dark slime. Oh, SNAP.

Willow _pushed his slime to the side to make room for_
her _potion of water breathing, and he pushed back._
I _thought the lovebirds were going to duke it out_
right _there in the middle of the swamp! I sat back to_
watch, _wishing I had a bucket of popcorn._

But then, for some reason, they both turned on ME.

"Aren't you trying to sell rap songs tonight?" Willow asked. I guess she wondered why I was sitting down instead of leaping over the counter, trying to bring in customers.

I shrugged. See, I'd figured out that I didn't HAVE to sell any rap songs. I was earning money just sitting there. Every time someone bought a bottle of potion or a hunk of slime, I could practically HEAR those emeralds plinking into my piggy bank.

New! Glow in t

Then Sam asked me how much I was going to chip in on his new tablet. I guess he's counting his emeralds at home too, wondering how soon he can head on over to the Mob Mall.

Well, I told Sam I couldn't chip in just yet—that I wanted to re-invest my emeralds "back into the business" first. What did that mean? I don't even know. I swear, this stuff just comes to me.

Genius!

But Willow busted me. "How are you re-investing in the business?" she asked.

I inspected the stand and said something like, "I've been thinking about giving this thing a coat of paint."

Well, Sam seemed satisfied with that. And when a bunch of zombies came over to buy some of Willow's potions, she finally backed off. PHEW.

So I'd have to call that another successful night for Gerald Creeper Jr. Incorporated. Time to log my earnings:

Daily Sales

· Bottles of potions sold: 12

· Homemade slime balls sold: 9

· Rap songs sold: 0

· Total sales: 105 emeralds

· My cut: 21 emeralds

I already have almost 40 emeralds. If sales keep going like this, I'll be able to buy my parrot NEXT weekend. YAAASSSS!!!

I'm thinking I'd better visit Critters Unlimited tomorrow to make sure he's still there. And maybe hide his cage behind a big bag of birdseed or something so no one else buys him first.

Success is so close, I can almost taste it. And you know what it tastes like? A giant roasted porkchop, burned to a crisp. YUM!!!

Success!

DAY 12: WEDNESDAY

Okay, my parrot is right where I left him—on the shelf at Critters Unlimited. PHEW!

I had to sneak away from our sales stand to go visit him last night. I told Willow I was going shopping for paint so I could spruce up our stand, and that she could just swing by my house this morning to drop off my share of the emeralds. (She might have given me the stink-eye when I said that. Or maybe she just had gunpowder in her eyes from brewing so many splash potions.)

Anyway, I high-tailed it to Critters Unlimited. I practically sprinted, because I was SO afraid someone else had bought my bird. But there he was, strutting back and forth in his cage, bobbing his blue head up and down with every step.

I hung out with Pete for a LONG time. (That's what I decided to name him—Pete the Parrot.) When other mobs came by, I stepped in front of his cage so no one else would see him and fall in love with him. I just whistled and pretended to be checking out the birdseed and bird toys on the shelf next to Pete.

And guess what? Pete whistled right back at me. He re-PEAT-ed every note!

So then I started rapping, just to see if he'd do that too.

Well, Pete got PART of the rap anyway. (We still have some work to do.) But now I know he's the bird for me. And I can't WAIT to bring him home.

It's time to earn some serious emeralds, FAST. I hope Sam and Willow are prepared to put in some overtime, because Gerald Creeper Jr. Incorporated is open for business—24 hours a day, 7 days a week.

DAY 14: FRIDAY

It's official: Dad can NEVER tell me again that I don't know the value of an emerald.

I have been working my creeper butt off for TWO STRAIGHT NIGHTS now. And I am one tired creeper. But I am also one RICH creeper!

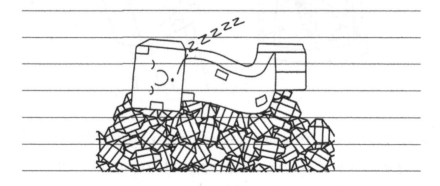

See, I had another brilliant idea. I decided Sam, Willow, and I should set up our selling stand where mobs are already going to shop—the Mob Mall. We found a spot in the parking lot by the front door, and we caught mobs before they even set foot in the mall (you know, while they still had emeralds in their pockets).

I even took a turn selling at the counter so Sam could run back to his house and get more slime balls, and so that Willow could take potion-brewing breaks. I earned EVERY one of my emeralds, let me tell you. By the end of the first night, my feet were sore from standing and my tongue was tied in knots from talking to customers so much.

But I didn't mind at all, because I earned 52 emeralds that night. Count them—52!!! And now, after another night, I have a pile of emeralds so big, they wouldn't fit in TEN piggy banks.

So I know you're wondering: Do I finally have enough emeralds to buy Pete the Parrot? Well, YES I do, thanks for asking. And if the mall weren't closed right now, I'd walk straight there to get Pete—even though my feet feel like blocks of obsidian.

But if I'm going to buy Pete tomorrow, I'm gonna have to do it on the sly.

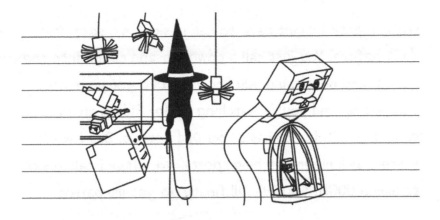

I can't buy _him_ in front of Willow and Sam, because
I'm SUPPOSED to be using my hard-earned emeralds
to "re-invest in the business." I _promised_ Willow I'd
paint the stand, and come up with a new chalkboard
sign that says Potion of the Day. She wants to
advertise one special potion every day of the
week. "But YOU should buy the chalkboard, Gerald,
because it's your stand and all," she pointed out.

"I'll get right on that," I told Willow. (I mean,
right after I buy my parrot, and teach him to rap,
and make a video that goes viral.) Anyway, Willow
doesn't have to worry. I have enough emeralds to
buy Pete PLUS a few "investments."

But tonight? I might have to call in sick. I've seen Dad do it before. You just call a coworker and cough into the phone, and next thing you know, you've got your feet propped up and you're watching Spider Riding on TV or something. At least that's how Dad does it. But I won't waste a sick night watching sports. No, after I call in sick to Sam (COUGH, COUGH), I'll finally go get my parrot.

Cough!
Cough!

Right after I get a good day's sleep. And soak my sore feet. And rest my voice (because you can't teach a parrot to rap if you can't even talk). I wonder if Mom has a cure for THAT in her Restore Your Health bag of tricks.

I'd go ask her right now. I mean, if I weren't SO t-i-r-e-d . . .

DAY 15: SATURDAY

Pete the Parrot is mine, all MINE!

It was NOT easy to sneak into Mob Mall without Willow and Sam seeing me. Those mobs must have gotten up at the crack of dusk to set up our stand early. And they were right by the front door, which meant I had to go in disguise. (I crouched down low and crept in with a bouncy family of slimes.)

Pete was right there waiting for me at Critters Unlimited. But I'd kind of forgotten a few things. Like, you can't just buy a parrot without a cage. Or without birdseed. What's the bird supposed to eat? Porkchops, burned to a crisp?

So I had to spend all my EXTRA emeralds too—which means Willow might not get her chalkboard sign any time soon.

I'd kind of forgotten something else, too—to ask my parents if I could bring Pete home. I mean, I figured I had that covered during the whole "emeralds don't grow on trees, Gerald" and "you have to get a job, son" conversation. But Mom didn't seem to remember any of that.

When I got home, she had her head stuck in the refrigerator. I asked, "What's for dinner?"

And then Pete did too.

I guess Pete's voice kind of freaked Mom out. She blew sky high, leaving the refrigerator full of gunpowder. And after she pulled herself together, she said we'd be having a whole lot of NOTHING for dinner, thanks to me and "that dirty bird." OOPS.

Things didn't go so well with Sticky either. As soon as I brought Pete into my room, Sticky squirted ink at him (or at least into his aquarium). RUDE. So I had to give Sticky a timeout in Chloe's room.

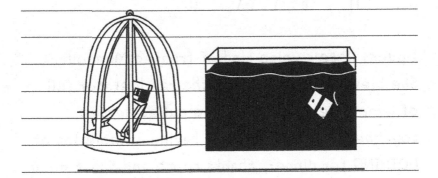

While I was in Chloe's room, I grabbed the phone that we're supposed to share (even though Chloe pretty much hogs it). Then I got to work teaching Pete how to rap. I've been waiting for a parrot for SO long now (two WHOLE WEEKS!), so I didn't want to waste another second.

When we'd finally made up a decent rap, I took a quick video. (It's not my best work, but it's a start, right?) Then I posted it straight to MooTube. Most of the videos there are of mooshrooms, ocelots, and other critters, so I know my rapping parrot is going to be a BIG hit.

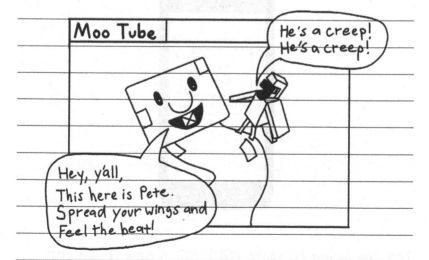

Now I'm sitting back and waiting for the likes to pour in!

Still waiting.

Okay, it's been like seven minutes now. STILL waiting.

Twelve minutes. SERIOUSLY? What's not to love about a rapping parrot?

Just heard a DING. Yaasssss! We got a thumbs-up!

They're going to start POURING in now, I can tell. But in the meantime, I'm just going to keep looking at that one thumb over and over again.

Uh-oh. I just looked closer. And I RECOGNIZE that thumb.

It's from Willow W. Loves the Swamp.

DING!

CRUD.

My ONE like is from the ONE mob that I didn't want to see this video. The mob who will bust my butt for not spending my emeralds on paint and a chalkboard sign. Which means that tomorrow, when I get to work, I'm going to have some serious explaining to do.

SIGH.

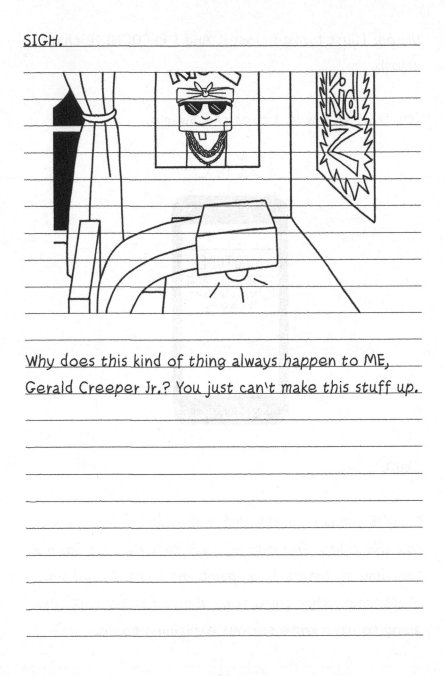

Why does this kind of thing always happen to ME,
Gerald Creeper Jr.? You just can't make this stuff up.

DAY 16: SUNDAY

So I spent the rest of last night trying to figure out
what I was going to say to Willow about that parrot.
That I'd BORROWED him from a friend? That he'd
flown through my window while I was in bed, trying
to sleep off my cold (SNIFFLE, SNIFFLE)? That I'd
gotten a visit from Kid Z himself, who thought I was
on my death bed and wanted to make my dying wish
of a rapping parrot come true?

Before I could come up with a halfway decent story,
the doorbell rang. Then Mom knocked on my door to
introduce a "visitor." Was it Kid Z?

Nope.

It was WILLOW.

I tried to pretend like everything was normal. "Willow, old buddy, old pal! Are you coming to see how I'm doing? (COUGH, SNIFFLE, SNEEZE) Or, hey, are you bringing me my share of the emeralds from last night? (HAH-CHOO!)"

That was when Pete the Parrot piped in with his own "HAH-CHOO!"

HAH-CHOO

Willow took one look at Pete, and then she pulled a potion bottle out of her robes. I thought she was going to throw it at me—I really did. Instead, she set it on the table next to Pete. "Potion of healing," she said. "For your parrot and his, um, COLD."

HUH. Any other mob might think that was pretty nice of Willow. But I knew something was up.

"From now on," Willow said, "I'm going to pay you 20 percent of my profits in POTIONS, not emeralds. I mean, until you start re-investing in the business."

A-HA! There it was. Willow was going to hold back on giving me emeralds till I bought that paint and signs for our selling stand. So it was time for me to turn on the big brains again.

"I AM investing in the business," I said. "Pete is really good at advertising. Listen to this: Pete, say, "Get your ice-cold potions!"

I had to repeat it like eight times, but Pete finally caught on.

And guess what? Willow SMILED. Sort of anyway. "That could work," she said. "He might draw a few customers."

"That's what I'm SAYING!" I cried, as if I couldn't believe Willow would ever doubt me.

As she was leaving, I thought about asking her again about my emeralds. I mean, I'd just come up with a pretty genius way to sell more of her potions, right? But when Willow is mad, it's good to just let her cool down for a while. And besides, I'd get my emeralds tonight from Sam.

And then? I'd buy Willow her sign and some white paint, and every employee in Gerald Creeper Jr. Incorporated would be happy again.

Before I went to bed, I checked MooTube to see if I'd gotten any more likes.

Nope. Not a single one.

So I guess this going viral thing takes time. (SIGH.)

But while I waited, something AMAZING happened. This ad popped up on my phone. Now usually those ads are for dumb things like "Miracle pills to help you lose a little gunpowder!" But this ad was different. It was like it was sent JUST FOR ME.

Here's what it looked like:

Now I don't know HOW the Elytra Wing company knew I had a parrot. But I clicked right on that ad to find out how much those wings cost.

129 emeralds plus tax.

HUH.

Time to dust off my 30-Day Plan, because I can check a few things off that list—and add a shiny NEW one.

30-Day Plan for
Getting a Rapping Parrot

~~Get a job that does NOT involve pigs, llamas, hard labor, or sweating.~~ (CHECK)

~~Earn 150 emeralds 110 emeralds (because I'll get 110 emeralds for allowance this month)~~ (CHECK)

~~Buy my parrot down at Critters Unlimited.~~ (CHECK)

· Teach that bird to rap, just like Kid Z's! (CHECK. Well, ALMOST check. I mean, Pete's still learning...)

But why stop there? Here's one more:

· Make a video of my rapping parrot, sit back, and WATCH it go viral. (CHECK, CHECK, and wait, I'd better check again... Nope. Not viral yet.)

· Earn 129 emeralds so I can buy Elytra Wings and fly sky-high with Pete!!!

I'll tell you what now. This getting-a-job thing is working out pretty well for me. Dad sure knows what he's talking about. I should have quit school and gone to work a LONG time ago.

I can hardly wait to get back out there tonight and SELL SOME STUFF. Time to refill my piggy banks—you know, so I can empty them out again. Elytra Wings, here I come!

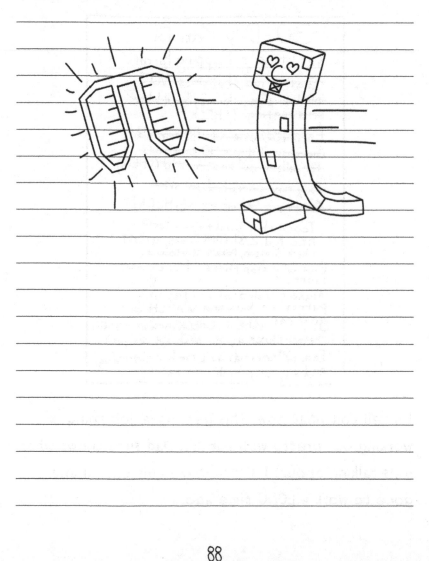

DAY 17: MONDAY

SHEESH. You do a friend a favor, and it ends up
biting you in the butt.

I mean, I advertised Willow's potions ALL NIGHT
LONG. Well, Pete did anyway. "Get your ice-cold
potions here!" he squawked at every mob who came
out of the mall.

Creepers crept, Endermen teleported, and zombies
staggered over JUST to see the talking bird. And
Willow RAKED in those emeralds. One potion of
swiftness? Coming right up. Three potions of

strength? You've got it—would you like a bag for that? Yup, Pete was a selling machine.

Sam was kind of bummed because Pete wasn't advertising his slime. But what can I say? You can only teach a parrot so much in a day. And besides, I figured I was going to get my emeralds either way.

Except . . . I DIDN'T.

Because this morning, as we were packing up, Willow handed me a potion bottle. "Your cut," she said. She didn't even let me CHOOSE which one I wanted.

What was I supposed to do with a potion of fire resistance?

"Um, what about my emeralds?" I said.

She reminded me that she wouldn't be giving me any emeralds until she got her chalkboard sign. "A deal's a deal," she said.

So THAT's how it was gonna be, huh?

I *thought* Sam would back me up, but I should have known better. Remember what I said about that three-wheeled minecart? Yup, he rolled right out of the stand after Willow and didn't even give me HIS emeralds.

When I asked *him* about them, he was all like, "I think I should keep them and *put them* toward my new tablet. Because, I mean, you SAID you'd chip in on it . . ."

WOW. You hire a few friends to help them out, and they turn on you like zombie pigmen.

So I told Sam and Willow that Pete and I were going home. And that tomorrow, Pete would be helping ME sell my RAP songs, thank you very much.

I _thought_ Sam called something back to me, but it was just Pete squawking.

He's a creep!
He's a creep!

I mean, I'm glad I still have ONE friend left, but he doesn't always say the most supportive things.

When I got home this morning, I decided to teach Pete a new sales pitch.

So far, it's not going so well. It could be a LONG sleepless day. (SIGH)

DAY 18: TUESDAY

You do not even WANT to know how things went last night.

But I'm going to tell you anyway, because if a creep can't tell his journal about the worst night EVER, who can he tell?

NOT his pet squid, who has been giving him the cold, wet shoulder since he brought home a parrot.

And NOT his parrot, who is nothing but a traitor.

"You hear that Pete?" I said. "You're a TRAITOR."

And you know what he said back to me?

Sometimes I wonder if Willow is sneaking in here
during the day while I sleep, and paying off my
parrot in bird treats to make him keep saying that.

Anyway, I wouldn't put anything past Willow
anymore. Do you know what she did? She started
selling potions from her OWN stand.

You can't even call it a stand, really. It's just a
table. That just happens to have a huge chalkboard
sign hanging from it. That says Get Your Potion of
the Night! in big annoying letters.

Get Your Potion
~of the Night~

I can't believe she went and got her own stand!
When I told her that was probably illegal, she said
she hadn't signed a CONTRACT with me. That she was
a free agent, whatever that means.

So while I was trying to sell rap songs from my
stand, Willow was selling a TON of potions from
hers. And Sam was kind of bouncing back and
forth between us, like he didn't know what else
to do.

As for Pete the Parrot? Well, he was sitting on MY shoulder, selling WILLOW's potions. Tonight, I'm leaving him home. Maybe I'll bring Sticky the Squid instead. At least my squid knows how to keep his mouth SHUT.

Guess what Willow's Potion of the Night was? Potion of SLOWING. And that's exactly what she was doing to me—slowing down my earnings. I'd NEVER get the Elytra Wings at this rate.

When Ziggy Zombie made an appearance, I practically tackled him.

> Want a rap song, Ziggy? For you, it's just five emeralds—my Friends and Family discount.

Ziggy looked confused. "Aren't your rap songs ALWAYS five emeralds?" he asked.

Every once in a while, the zombie makes a good point. So I told him I'd give him TWO raps for the price of one: one for him, and one for Zoe, who was riding her chicken in circles around Ziggy's legs.

But Ziggy said he couldn't buy a rap song because he'd ALREADY spent his allowance on the Potion of the Night. Then, right in front of me, he opened up that potion of slowness and splashed some of it on Zoe.

Well, that baby zombie slowed down right away—as if she'd just ridden her chicken into a river of hot lava. "Now I can keep up with her!" said Ziggy with a sigh of relief. "Best emeralds I ever spent."

So it looked like Willow was getting PLENTY of sales without me. Maybe she didn't need my big brains after all.

And Sam? He kept inching closer and closer to Willow's stand. So finally I told him just to GO already. Then I packed up and left too. What was the point?

Get Your Potion
~of the Night~

When I got home, I was ready to blow (and I'm not really the exploding kind of creeper). Sam and Willow just made me SO mad. With friends like that, who needs enemies? I might as well have hired a couple of ghasts from the Nether.

I couldn't even eat my breakfast this morning. I just pushed my crispy potatoes around and around on my plate till Mom asked what was wrong. So I told her— EVERYTHING. And you know what Dad said?

He said that it was GOOD that Willow and Sam had their own stand.

SHEESH. Where does he even come UP with this stuff?

Well, Mom had my back. Turns out, Cora Creeper's mom started working as a sales rep for Restore Your Health Incorporated, TOO, only she didn't sign up under Mom. She signed up under some witch from the swamp. And Mom does NOT appreciate that kind of competition.

So Mom and I gave Dad the stink-eye all during breakfast. And afterward, I went right to my room and slammed the door.

But I couldn't stop thinking about what Dad had said. (I really hate it when that happens.) And I started to think the old man might be right about something.

I DID have to work harder. Well, maybe not HARDER, but SMARTER. Because I didn't have coworkers anymore. And my rap songs weren't exactly flying off the shelves. But that didn't mean I couldn't sell SOMETHING ELSE.

I need to come up with something that costs almost NOTHING to make, but that I can sell for a lot of emeralds. See, THAT'S smart business.

Anyway, I'm going to sleep on it, because sometimes my biggest, BEST ideas come to me in the middle of the day.

Wish me luck.

DAY 19: WEDNESDAY

Sometimes a bad idea can turn into a GOOD idea if it comes along at the right time.

At least that's what I thought about my Super Deluxe Hot Chocolate with whipped cream and sprinkles. I mean, when Sam had the idea to sell hot chocolate, it was bad. Because, you know, Sam can't eat whipped cream without getting gassy, and caffeine makes him weird.

But that doesn't mean that I, Gerald Creeper Jr., can't sell hot cocoa, right?

So last night, I left Pete at home (next to Sticky—I think it's time those two make friends). And I brought a bunch of stuff from Mom's cabinets to make the BEST hot chocolate ever.

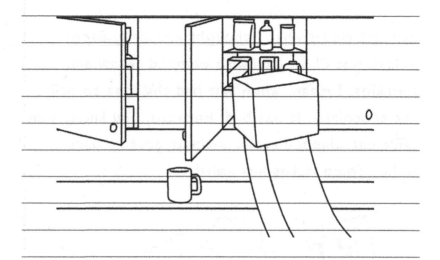

But you know what I saw as soon as I got to the selling stand? I saw two MORE selling stands. Turns out, Willow isn't the only mob who got the idea to sell her own stuff.

Cora Creeper was standing by a barrel selling GUNPOWDER. And was that Chloe beside her?

SERIOUSLY? My Evil Twin was trying to steal my business?

When I made a stink about it, Chloe pointed out that we were selling DIFFERENT things. Which I guess is true. So while she was advertising her deal on gunpowder, I hollered even louder to get people to buy hot chocolate.

Willow didn't HAVE to say anything to customers. Her chalkboard said it for her. And Sam? Well, he'd brought some "advertising" of his own—a mini trampoline. And that trampoline really drew a crowd, let me tell you.

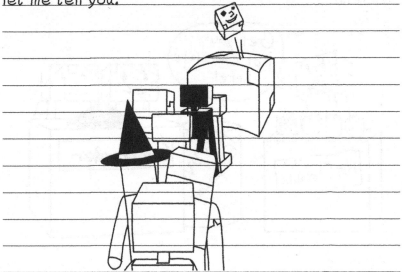

Did I mention that after mobs wear themselves out on a trampoline, they do NOT reach for a hot beverage? The only mob who came over to buy hot chocolate was Sam himself. And that lactose-intolerant slime ordered EXTRA whipped cream. GREAT.

So maybe I won't bring hot chocolate again tomorrow night. I mean, there's plenty of other good ideas where that one came from, right? I just have to keep thinking on it—and try to STOP thinking about how much I want to jump on Sam's mini trampoline . . .

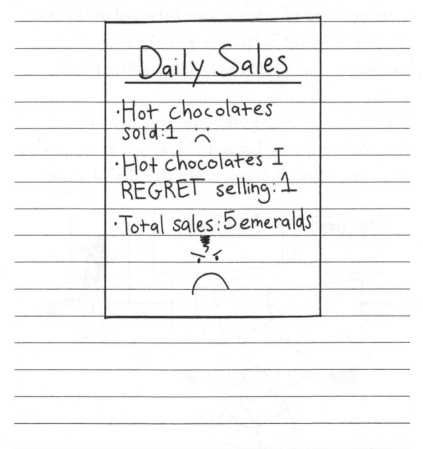

DAY 20: THURSDAY

Last night I took a mental-health break. That's what Mom calls it when she doesn't do any work and does FUN stuff instead.

I was going to stay home with Pete and Sticky, and try to make a rap video with both of them in it—something that would really light up MooTube.

But instead, I found myself creeping down to the Mob Mall to spy on Sam and Willow—you know, just to see how things were going. And GUESS what I saw?

Even MORE stands and MORE mobs selling stuff.
Ziggy Zombie had his own stand, which looked like a
pigpen full of baby mobs. I guess he figured that if
grown-ups were hitting the mall, they might need a
place to drop off their baby zombies and creepers.

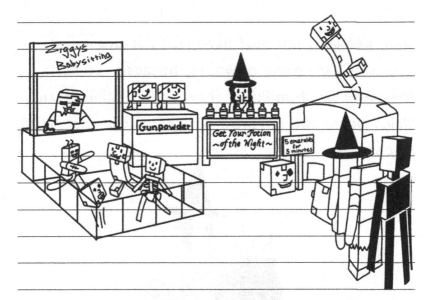

Now I don't know WHAT mob would hire a zombie
to babysit, but it sure looked like business was
booming. Ziggy was raking in the emeralds. So were
Cora and Chloe with their gunpowder sales, and Sam
had a whole LINE of mobs waiting to jump on his mini
trampoline. He was even charging admission for it
now: 5 emeralds for 5 minutes.

I'd call it genius, but I really don't like to throw that word around. Sam might get an even BIGGER head than he already has.

And Willow?

Well, get this: she must have really struck it rich over the last couple of weeks, because she has a shiny new cauldron RIGHT there in her selling stand. Which means she can brew potions on the spot. LOTS of potions.

Get Your Potion
~of the Night~

So here's what I want to know: WHERE are mobs getting all these emeralds to spend on slime,

112

potions, and gunpowder? I mean, what kind of an ALLOWANCE are they getting? And why didn't MY parents get the memo about giving kids a raise?

Let me tell you, life is just getting more unfair by the second.

I came home this morning to complain to Dad about it, but you know what I found when I walked through the door?

Mom was SINGING. It doesn't happen very often, but when it does, everything STOPS. The ground rumbles. Glass shatters. Pete the Parrot squawks. And poor Sticky had his tentacles stuck to his ears.

When I asked Mom if she could take it down a notch, I noticed something. Her teeth were BLACK as gunpowder. She looked so creepy, I jumped sky-high.

When I worked up the courage to look Mom in the face and ask her about it, she said she was celebrating record sales of her new TOP-selling product: Charcoal Tooth-Whitening Powder.

Say WHAT now?

Mom showed me how many bottles she had sold already. "It's flying out of my case," she said. She smiled wide with those coal-black teeth. YIKES.

I guess some online ad has been telling mobs that they can get "300 percent whiter teeth" by using the stuff. But what I want to know is, how can something BLACK make your teeth WHITE? I mean, mobs might as well be spending their emeralds on gunpowder! At least you can make FIREWORKS out of that.

So I'm trying to go to sleep now, but I keep picturing Mom with her scary black teeth. Even Sticky is sleeping with one tentacle covering his eyes, like he can't bear to look. And I had to throw a blanket over Pete's birdcage to quiet him down after all that singing and squawking.

I sure hope I don't have daymares of Mom, looking like an undead mob with black, rotten teeth. (Of course, now that I'm thinking about it, I WILL.)

And how am I supposed to come up with my next genius sales idea if I can't get any decent SLEEP???

DAY 20: THURSDAY (CONTINUED)

YES!!! Genius strikes again!!! And I have a horrible
daymare to THANK for it!

I dreamt that a zombie pigman was chasing me
across the schoolyard, trying to hit me with
its sword. Except it WASN'T a sword. It was a
ginormous bottle of Charcoal Tooth-Whitening
Powder. And it wasn't a zombie pigman. It was
MOM, with a gaping black hole where her mouth
used to be. YIKES!!!

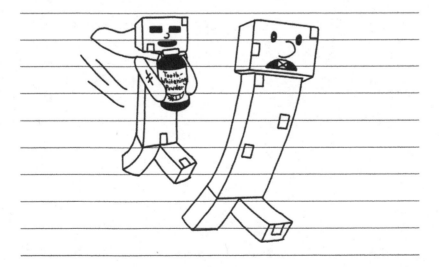

When she threw the bottle at me, it exploded, and I was COVERED in black powder. Except it wasn't tooth-whitening powder—it was GUNpowder. And then Chloe was next to me with this evil grin, and she started striking flint against steel. She was trying to light me on fire!

That's when I exploded. Except instead of just falling to pieces in a cloud of gunpowder, I shot sky-high. I was flying—with Elytra Wings. And all the gunpowder that was raining down on the Overworld turned into FIREWORKS—beautiful, colorful fireworks.

When I woke up, I had this HUGE smile on my face. There's nothing better than when a daymare turns into the best dream EVER.

And the best IDEA ever.

See, it came to me just like that—my next sales idea. I'm going to sell FIREWORKS!!!

I can't believe I didn't think of it before. I mean, I'm really GOOD at making fireworks. I even have a medal to prove it from the Overworld Games last year. And the Fourth of July is coming, so mobs will be ALL OVER my fireworks stand.

If Chloe hasn't used up all the gunpowder Dad stores in the garage, I can start making fireworks RIGHT NOW. And maybe even have some tonight to sell!

Who needs sleep?

Not THIS genius creep!!!

DAY 21: FRIDAY

Okay, my eyes are drooping shut as I write this. I might fall asleep face first in my journal. But I GOTTA try to get some of this down, because when I'm rich and famous, I'll look back on last night and write speeches about it and stuff. "The Moment It All Turned Around," I'll call it. And my speeches will inspire little creepers everywhere NEVER to give up on their dreams.

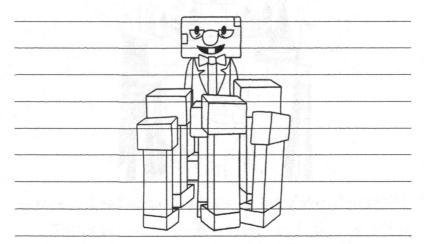

But back to yesterday. See, I DID stay up all day making fireworks. I made long ones. Fat ones. Striped ones. Fireworks that twinkle. Fireworks that explode in the shape of a star. Fireworks that explode in the shape of a CREEPER!

I'd learned how to do ALL of that during the Overworld Games. Sometimes, a creeper's just gotta fall back on what he KNOWS, and then watch the emeralds pour in . . .

By the time I got to the mall last night, I was pushing a minecart FULL of fireworks. And all those other mobs trying to sell their goods saw me coming from a mile away, let me tell you.

Willow's eyes got wide. Sam bounced over to see what was up. Ziggy even left his baby mobs unattended while he staggered over to see my cart—until a baby Enderman started crying and teleported OUT of the pen.

Chloe looked especially suspicious. I'll bet my Evil Twin was mad she hadn't used up the last of the gunpowder from the garage. Because who was going to buy her boring old gunpowder now, when they could buy firework rockets STUFFED with gunpowder?

Mobs lined up to see what kind I had. Even grown-up mobs stopped by to pick up fireworks for their kids for the Fourth of July.

As the emeralds poured in, I had to kick myself a
couple of times to make sure I wasn't dreaming.
I mean, I WAS really tired. And it's possible I fell
asleep a couple of times in between customers. But
it was ALL worth it when I counted my earnings.

Daily Sales

•Firework rockets
sold: 19

•Total sales: 95
emeralds

WOOT-WOOT!

And I deserve every single one of those emeralds.
I mean, I've been working REALLY hard. It's about
TIME some of that started paying off, right?

(Sorry—drool spot here. I'm SO tired!!!)

I'm going to bed now. And when I wake up tonight,
I'm gonna celebrate with Pete. Because really SOON,
my bird and I are going to be flying side by side.

Those Elytra Wings have my name written ALL over them.

And I know exactly what I'm going to dream about today.

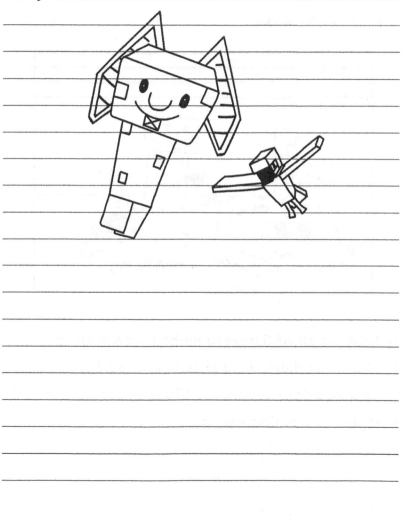

127

DAY 23: SUNDAY

WHEW!!!

No time to write. No time to rap. All I've been doing is work, work, WORK.

It took me all of Saturday night to make more fireworks. It didn't help that Chloe used up the gunpowder—or at least STOLE it out of the garage so I couldn't use it.

But I have a secret weapon. See, I can be
SUPER annoying. I know *how to push* my Evil
Twin's buttons to make her explode on the spot
(the creeper has a seriously short fuse). PRESTO!
Then I just grab the broom and dustpan, and
sweep up the gunpowder. Which makes Chloe mad
enough to blow up again (giving me DOUBLE the
payout).

When Chloe finally caught on to me and stormed
out of the house, I decided to hang out with my

baby sister, Cammy. That baby explodes when she's mad but ALSO when she's HAPPY. Or laughing. Or surprised. Or really excited. That's pretty much why we call her the Exploding Baby.

After I rapped and made her baby dolls dance, she blew up with laughter—and donated to my gunpowder stash too. SCORE!!!

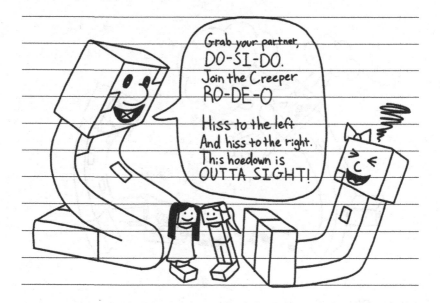

After all that quality sister time, I holed up in the garage to work. I even tried to make myself blow up once or twice, just to eke out a little more gunpowder. But like I said, I'm not really the exploding kind of creeper. So I decided to stick to what I know best and just finish up those fireworks.

Then last night, I hauled them to the mall and prepped for ANOTHER stellar night of sales. I was SURE I'd be able to buy my Elytra Wings after just one more night.

But then I happened to sneak a peek at Willow's chalkboard sign as I passed, and what she'd written was a real shocker, let me tell you.

Well, I'm no DUMMY. I knew exactly what she was doing. She was piggybacking off my sales! For every firework rocket I sold, she tried to sell a potion of fire resistance too. "Just in case a firework blows up unexpectedly," she told a mob who had bought one of my rockets. And "So you don't lose any fingers," she told another. Or "To keep your children SAFE," she told a zombie mother.

Well, talk about SCARING OFF customers. One mob mother was heading my way, until she overheard

Willow's sales _pitch._ Then she turned right around
and headed to buy potions instead.

ARRRGGGHH!!!

I marched over to Willow and told her to STOP, but
she went on and on about how she was just "filling
a customer need" now that I was putting all those
dangerous fireworks out into the Overworld. Then
she had the nerve to say that I should buy some of
her potion of fire resistance, too. "You know, just
in case something blows up in your stand," she said.

AS IF I would ever give her a single emerald for her
potions. Willow _must_ have known I wasn't buying her
line, because she said maybe we should just make a

trade—one firework rocket for one of her bottles of fire resistance.

"Ah, no thanks," I said. But now I know the TRUTH. Willow secretly WANTS one of my rockets! And guess what? She's not going to get one. Not if she keeps scaring away my customers with her fire-safety warnings.

So GAME ON, Willow. Tonight, I'm pulling out all the stops. I'm bringing Pete the Parrot to lure in customers. I'm going to GIVE AWAY free hot chocolate. And my best idea yet? I'm going to fight fire with fire—fireWORKS, that is.

I'm going to give customers a DEMO of my fireworks.
I'll light up one of those rockets and send it
through the sky right over the mall. That way, NO
ONE will listen to Willow's warnings. They'll be too
WOWED by my fireworks show!

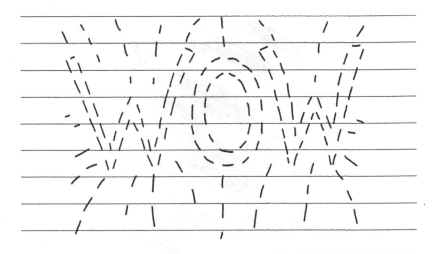

GENIUS. Pure genius. Sometimes a big-ideas guy
even wows HIMSELF.

DAY 24: MONDAY

DO. NOT. ASK.

Don't ask me what those black smudges are all over the page.

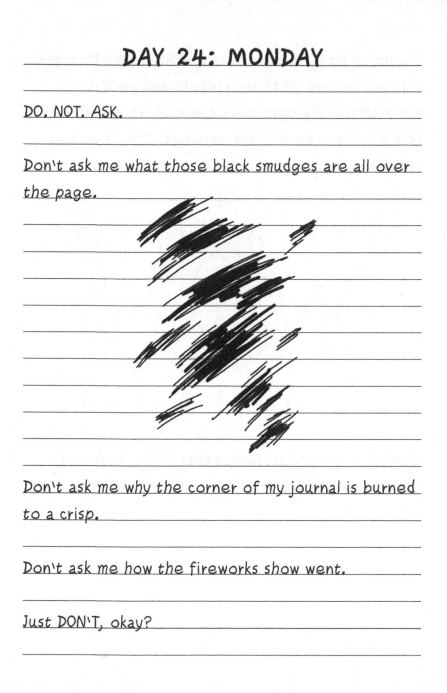

Don't ask me why the corner of my journal is burned to a crisp.

Don't ask me how the fireworks show went.

Just DON'T, okay?

Because I mean, if you did, then I'd have to tell you how the rocket that I lit went straight up in the air. And came straight back down. And landed in my stash of other firework rockets.

HAPPY 4th OF JULY!

I'd have to tell you how it BURST into flames. And lit all those other rockets on fire. And lit my STAND on fire.

I'd have to tell you how my stand burned to a crisp, right in front of my eyes. And took all my hopes and dreams with it.

And I'd have to tell you that Pete the Parrot is GONE. He flew the coop when all those fireworks went off. And it's ALL MY FAULT.

Oh, Pete, old buddy, old pal. Did you get hurt? Did you fly away? WHERE ARE YOU???

I looked in Ziggy's babysitting stand. I looked under every minecart in the mall parking lot. I walked around the WHOLE mall. But there was no sign of my bird. Not a single feather.

So now I've got NOTHING. No fireworks. No stand. No rapping parrot.

Nothing but Sticky the Squid, who is staring at me, wondering what I'm going to do next.

Oh, and now I've got a pile of emeralds for my piggy bank that I was GOING to use to buy Elytra Wings. But what good are wings if I don't have a parrot to fly with?

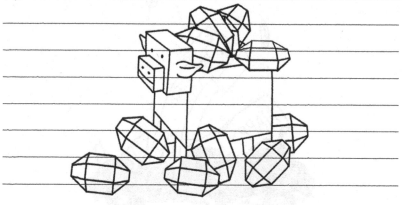

"Are you gonna buy a new parrot?" Sam texted me this morning.

SERIOUSLY???

I mean, what does Sam think? That I can just waltz down to Critters Unlimited and replace Pete with another bird? Maybe I should go to the mall and buy a new BEST FRIEND too. That's what I wanted to say. But I tried to pull it together. I mean, the slime was probably trying to be nice.

I guess there are just some things emeralds can't buy. Add THAT to Dad's list of brilliant sayings.

Now, all I have left of Pete is the rap video we made when I first brought him home. So excuse me while I go watch that again for like the trillionth time.

Oh, and if you hear a sniffle or two, don't say a word. It's probably just Sticky, who has been missing his buddy Pete. And I don't care what anyone says— it's perfectly OKAY for squid to cry.

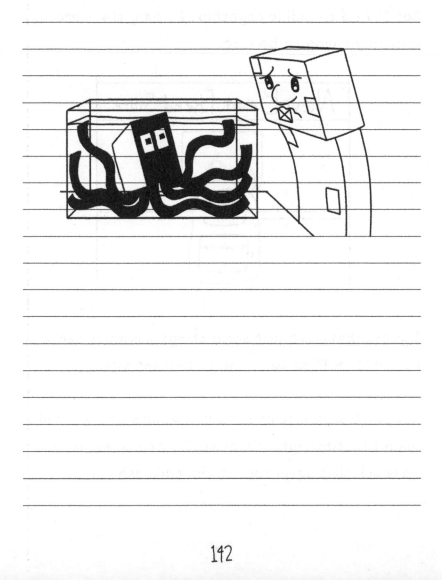

DAY 25: TUESDAY

MAN. Just when a creep thinks things can't get any worse.

Get this: Chloe came home from the mall this morning, and she says Willow and Sam are MAD at me. Even Ziggy Zombie is mad at me (and I'm pretty sure that's a first).

WHY are they mad, you ask? Well, that's a really good question. That's what I asked too. So Chloe went right ahead and told me.

I guess my fireworks show "alerted" the grown-ups to what was going on in the Mob Mall parking lot. Some Enderman came to the parking lot and shut down the rest of the stands. The Enderman said that the kids didn't have PERMITS to sell that stuff, and that it could be dangerous for them to be out there like that.

REALLY???

So Chloe says my friends are mad at ME for drawing attention to their market. They blame me for all the emeralds that they're NOT going to earn over the rest of the summer. And she said Sam is especially upset because now he won't earn enough for his new tablet.

Well, I pointed out to Chloe that if Sam and Willow hadn't been traitors and set up their own stand, I wouldn't have had to sell fireworks in the first place. We'd still be the only stand in the parking lot, and we'd have ALL those emeralds for ourselves.

But Chloe didn't want to hear it. I guess she's siding with the rest of them.

FINE. I don't need friends. Just add them to the list of everything else I lost this summer.

Pretty much the only mob who understands (besides Sticky) is Mom. Turns out, she got burned with her business, too. Mobs started complaining that the Charcoal Tooth-Whitening Powder was staining their teeth BLACK. (Well, DUH. I could have told them that.) And they all want their emeralds back. Poor

Mom is having to shell out her OWN emeralds just to satisfy the line of crabby mobs at the front door.

She's out back right now, burning the rest of her charcoal powder. I guess she figured if she can't sell it, she might as well burn the trash with it. So Mom's business went up in smoke, just like mine.

I'd go out and roast marshmallows over her fire, except I'm not hungry. Not even sort of, which is pretty weird for a creeper like me.

I tried playing some Humancraft, but even freaking out all those tiny humans in my videogame didn't make me feel better.

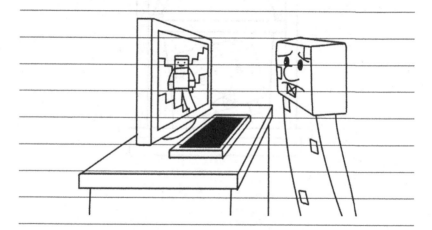

I guess I'm what they call DEPRESSED. And there's no cure.

Except Pete the Parrot.

I'm leaving my window open, just in case he comes home. I'm going to sit here and stare out that window for as long as it takes. Why not? I mean, what else does a friendless, jobless, parrot-less creep have to do?

DAY 25: TUESDAY (CONTINUED)

So I had a glimmer of hope just now.

Yup, it flew right through my window on a gentle breeze.

I looked up from my pillow, and I SWEAR I saw Pete flapping his wings and heading toward my bed.

But . . .

. . . it turned out to be a piece of burned paper from Mom's firepit.

Story of my life. I hope for one thing, and instead I get a big old piece of TRASH.

So I'm starting to think it's time to throw my hope in the trash pit and let it burn. Time to face facts. Because here's the thing:

Pete's not coming home.

EVER.

DAY 26: WEDNESDAY

PETE CAME HOME!!!

YAAAAAASSSSSSSSSSSS!!!!!!

Well, Sam and Willow BROUGHT him home.

At first, I thought Willow had been hiding him all along, just to get back at me for outselling her potions with my fireworks. But Sam said they'd found Pete hopping around the Mob Mall parking lot when they went back to take down their stands. And Sam's not a slime who makes stuff up.

"He has a burned wing, see?" Sam said, lifting one of Pete's wings.

Pete's wing looked just fine to me (thank Golem). When I said so, Willow shrugged and said she'd used one of her potions of healing on it.

Well, that was pretty nice of her I guess. I told her thanks, and then the three of us sat around all awkward like. I mean, there's not much to say after you've been trying to outsell and outsmart each other all summer long.

Finally I mumbled, "Sorry about your stand getting shut down and all." I figured it was the least I could say, after they'd brought home my bird.

I thought Sam would tell me not to worry about it, because he's the kind of slime that bounces back after disappointment. But he didn't. He melted into one of his sad mopey pools.

Willow's the one who said, "Sam worked REALLY hard to get enough emeralds for that tablet, Gerald. And he got pretty close too."

Well, SHOOT. What did she want me to do? Pat the slime on the back? I'd worked hard, TOO. Was it MY fault that some grown-ups have nothing better to do than go around shutting down stands and spoiling kids' fun?

"Yes, it's absolutely, totally your fault." That's what Willow would have said if I'd argued. So I stuck with saying "sorry" again.

But SHEESH. I'd just gotten Pete back, and now my friends were really harshing my mellow.

When Sam and Willow finally left, I hugged on Pete for a while—you know, until he squawked. Then we celebrated his homecoming with a new rap, one I made up right there on the spot.

THIS time, Pete got the words right. So I guess that means HE's happy to be home too.

DAY 27: THURSDAY

It's funny _how_ EVERYTHING can change in a single night. Sometimes it goes from good to bad. (Like the night my fireworks stand exploded and ended up closing down all my friends' businesses, too. OOPS.) Other times it goes from bad to good. Like when Sam and Willow brought my parrot home.

Because I gotta tell you, I woke up tonight feeling GREAT. Like I could do ANYTHING.

I could build another stand. I could find another place to sell fireworks (or maybe, you know, something ELSE this time). I could buy those Elytra Wings and have them shipped overnight from the End City so they'd be here TOMORROW. Pete and I could be flying high above the Overworld in less than 24 hours!!!

I actually went online and found the wings. I clicked on them to put them in my shopping cart. I even called Mom into my room to see if I could give her emeralds in exchange for her buying the wings with her credit card.

But Pete kept interrupting us. "Pete is home! Pete is home!" I guess he was reminding me of the MOST important thing—that he was back. "Thanks to Sam and Willow," he squawked.

Well, he didn't really say that last part. But my ears heard it anyway—like my bird was scolding me for not remembering my friends.

What did he want me to DO? It's not like I had enough emeralds to buy wings for Sam and Willow too.

> But you have enough to help Sam buy his tablet.

> ?

Okay, that wasn't Pete talking. That must have been my conscience. Mom says there's this little voice in your head that tells you the RIGHT thing to do, even when you don't want to hear it.

I tried not to listen. I squeezed my eyes shut, as if THAT would help. But a conscience is kind of like

a squawking parrot. You can't make it be quiet—or make it say what you WANT it to say.

So when Mom asked what I wanted to buy online, I told her that . . . I'd changed my mind. (SIGH.)

After Mom left the room, I duked it out with my
conscience for about half an hour. But that little
dude is TOUGH! So finally I threw in the towel and
texted Sam. I offered to chip in on his new tablet.
Then I hit SEND before I could change my mind again.

Now I've got to count my emeralds. Because if Sam
and I have enough, my buddy and I are heading back
to Mob Mall—TONIGHT.

DAY 28: FRIDAY

You have never SEEN a slime as bouncy as Sam was when we came back from the Mob Mall last night. I had to tell him to settle down so he didn't BUST his brand-new tablet.

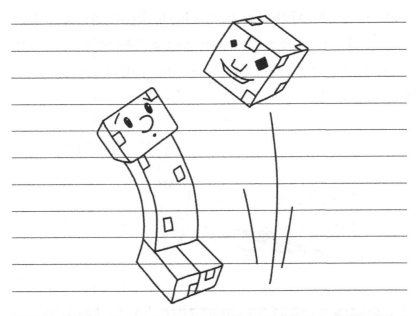

But I'll tell you what, those were the best emeralds I EVER spent. Sam keeps talking about everything we're going to do, now that he has a tablet again. I mean, sure, we'll take some videos of his cat, Moo. And Sam wants to make DIY slime videos too.

(I guess if he can't sell the stuff anymore, he at least wants to get famous for his special recipe.)

But Sam ALSO said he'd help me take videos of Pete the Rapping Parrot and post them on to his mom's special MooTube channel. Mrs. Slime posts lots of videos on MooTube of Sam's little brothers, and I guess the triplet mini slimes get a TON of likes. So if Mrs. Slime posts one of our rapping parrot videos on her channel, it could go viral for sure!

I'm pretty pumped up about that. So if I have to suffer through a goopy slime video or two first, NO worries. I'll survive.

In fact, now that I got my buddy Sam back, my big IDEAS are back too. Like last night, after I got back from the mall, I found Mom sorting through all her Restore Your Health Incorporated stuff. She said she isn't going to sell any more of it, because it ended up costing her more than she earned. So she's going to GIVE some of the stuff away to her friends.

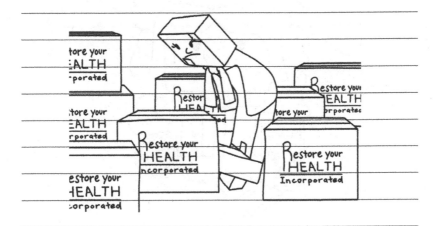

She pulled out a couple bottles of fish oil for Mrs. Zombie, because I guess it helps her peeling skin or something. (And zombies don't mind smelling like dead fish.) Then Mom pulled out a box of dandelion tea for Aunt Constance.

"Does Aunt Constance have a gas problem?" I asked, because you know, the tea is supposed to be good for stuff like that.

And Mom said NO, thanks for asking, and that Aunt Constance was going to use the dandelion tea to dye her yarn yellow for knitting.

"So you're just GIVING all this stuff away?" I asked. I couldn't stand the thought of Mom losing out on all those emeralds she should have been making.

But she just shrugged. "Mrs. Zombie will probably drop off some carrots and potatoes from her garden," she said. "You know, like a trade." Then her eyes lit up and she said something about Aunt Constance maybe knitting me a sweater.

Well, that was my cue to leave the kitchen. I've already got WAY too many ugly sweaters from Mom's knitting kick. The last thing I need is a bright dandelion-yellow sweater to add to my collection.

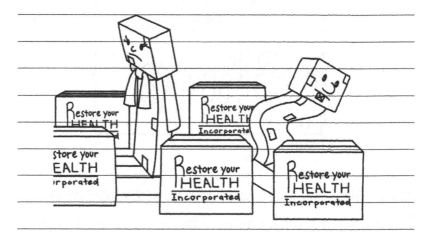

But Mom's dandelion tea got me to thinking. My genius brain fired up, and I thought about my buddy Sam, who always makes the SAME green slime. So I told Mom maybe I could bring a box of that tea to Sam so he could try a new color for a change. And she said sure.

That's how Sam and I ended up making a "Dandelion Slime" video. I mean, I was the behind-the-scenes camera guy, because slime is really Sam's thing. But after his mom posted the video, we got 41 likes JUST last night.

Moo Tube

Dandelion Slime

👍 41

You'd think Sam and I had earned 41 EMERALDS the way we were dancing around his living room! I kept thinking about how popular my rapping parrot was going to be, with the help of Sam's mom and her followers.

Sam kept saying thank you and asking if I wanted emeralds for that box of tea. "Because I might need more," he said, "to make more videos."

But I told Sam no—that he could consider that tea "interest" for what I owed him on the tablet. I don't even really know what that means, but Dad said it a couple of nights ago when Chloe asked for an advance on her allowance.

I guess Chloe's running out of emeralds now that she can't sell her gunpowder. And she's back to making homemade slime too. (In fact, I'm pretty sure I've got some of it stuck to the bottom of my foot right now.)

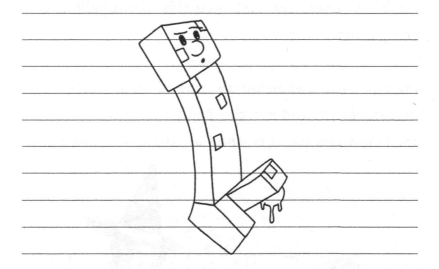

That's when my conscience struck again. "She'd still be selling her gunpowder if it weren't for your little fireworks disaster."

AAARRRGGGGHHHH!!!! How do I shut this dude up?

Finally I said, "Sam, there IS something I'd take in exchange for that tea. Maybe I could bring home a hunk of your Dandelion Slime for Chloe."

It wasn't any big thing. In fact, I don't even want to talk about it anymore. But let's just say that Chloe will go BANANAS when she sees that slime. And maybe my conscience will give this whole guilt-trip thing a rest.

Anyway, that's when Willow showed up at Sam's house. We showed her the Dandelion Slime video, thinking she'd be as pumped up about it as we were.

But Willow was in a funk. Even her nose drooped.

"What gives, Willow?" I finally asked, because I could tell she wanted me to.

She let out this ginormous sigh and said she missed the market. "What are we supposed to DO for the rest of the summer?" she said. "I have all these bottles of potion and not a single mob to sell them to. I can't even earn emeralds to buy new ingredients. I ran out of gunpowder this morning, so . . . no more splash potions for me."

Was she still trying to make me feel guilty for ruining the whole market thing at the mall? I dunno, but I had to put a stop to it—PRONTO.

"I'll get you some gunpowder," I promised her. "Chloe's got a ton of it. Maybe she'll trade me some of it for Dandelion Slime." (And, I mean, if she didn't, I could always hang out with Baby Cammy for a while and collect my own.)

Willow perked up after that, especially when Sam said maybe we could make a potion-brewing video to add to his mom's MooTube channel. I almost protested. I mean, when were we going to make MY rapping parrot video? I think the slime is kind of getting ahead of himself.

But that's okay. At least Sam and Willow are acting normal again. And hanging out with them sure beats sitting around, stewing about a lost bird, right? RIGHT.

So now I'm home, and it's time to go see a creeper twin about some gunpowder . . .

DAY 29: SATURDAY

Well, wonders never cease.

That's what my Grandpa Gerald used to say when something amazing happened. And those are the words that almost popped out of MY mouth when Chloe gave me a whole BARREL of gunpowder for Willow.

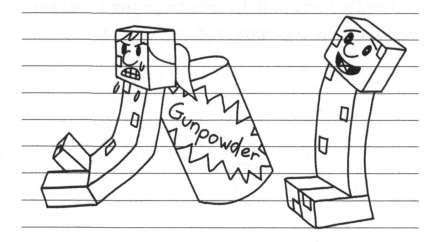

I think it's because Chloe was THRILLED with the Dandelion Slime. You'd think I just handed her the world's largest emerald or something. She stared at it, and stretched it, and nearly kissed it, I swear. Then she said I could have all the gunpowder I wanted, as long as I kept bringing her Sam's latest slime creations.

So I hauled that barrel off to Sam's, and went through that celebration fest all over again with Willow. She couldn't believe I'd give her that whole barrel of gunpowder for FREE.

She offered to give me potion in exchange for it, but I just kind of shrugged. I mean, it was Chloe's gunpowder, not mine. I was only the middleman. And besides, Willow DID bring home my parrot, safe and sound. So, whatever—we were even.

Then Willow said something like, "We all got what we wanted, didn't we?"

I guess we did. I got my rapping parrot. Sam got his tablet, plus an idea for a new kind of slime.

Willow got her new cauldron, plus gunpowder to brew more splash potions. Even Chloe got her Dandelion Slime.

But I'll admit, I'm the kind of creeper who has to have the last word. So I MIGHT have said something about not getting my Elytra Wings. I wasn't being crabby about it. It's just a fact.

I hopped online and showed the wings to Sam and Willow, and they thought they were pretty cool too. (I mean, who WOULDN'T???)

"Guess you'd better start saving your allowance," Willow said.

REALLY??? "Thanks, Mom," I joked.

Then I thought we were all done with that conversation. I ran home to get Pete the Parrot, because Sam said we were finally going to make my rapping parrot video. YAAASSSS!!!

But you know what happened?

Sam and Willow had a SURPRISE waiting for me when I got back to Sam's house. Willow handed it to me with a huge smile. "Potion of leaping," she said.

HUH?

"It won't make you FLY exactly," she said. "But you can leap pretty high."

Well, I couldn't WAIT to try that stuff out. I didn't even mind the nasty taste—I took a big swig.

Then I started to run. And my jog turned into a sprint. And then my steps turned into leaps. And pretty soon I felt like SuperCreep, able to leap tall buildings (or at least Sam's trampoline) in a single bound!

Pete the Parrot started flying after me, squawking. I think he was saying, "Wait for me! Wait for me!"

So I did. I waited just until my parrot landed on my shoulder, and then I took off again.

I could have kept leaping FOREVER, I swear. But when the potion wore off and I came back down to earth, I screwed the lid on that potion bottle and tucked it safely in my backpack. That's the kind of stuff you want to save, to make it last all summer.

I guess Sam got a VIDEO of my leaping too. He says he'll show me tomorrow.

So I'm in bed now, my legs still twitching after all that leaping. Pete looks pretty happy too, strutting around his cage. And I'm thinking Willow was right. We DID all kind of get what we wanted.

I mean, I didn't get those Elytra Wings. But the potion of leaping is pretty cool, and it cost a LOT less than those wings—no emeralds required. (So maybe I AM finally learning the value of an emerald. The old man would be proud.)

YAWN.

Gotta sleep now. More leaping and video-making to do tomorrow . . .

DAY 30: SUNDAY

Sometimes I wake up with Baby Cammy in my face. She crawls all over my head, laughing. It's not the best way to wake up, but it's not the WORST way either.

Tonight when I woke up, it was CHLOE in my face. And she was grinning like a geek. WHY?

"Your video went VIRAL!" she said.

181

HUH?

She shoved the phone in my face.

I expected to see my rapping parrot. Or maybe Sam's Dandelion Slime. Or even Willow's potion brewing. I mean, we'd made so many videos by now, it could have been any ONE of them.

Except it wasn't. It was some superhero creeper, soaring high above the ground with a . . . bird on his shoulder.

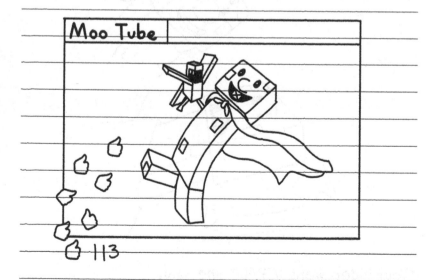

"That's ME!" I cried, grabbing the phone.

Sure enough, it was me and my parrot, leaping above Sam's backyard. And when I looked below the video, I saw it go up to 957 likes. Count them! 957!!!

I guess mobs have never seen a leaping creeper before. At least not one with a parrot sidekick.

I leaped right out of bed, no potion required. Why? Because I was wasting moonlight with every second I stayed in bed.

See, the way I figure it, I've got two months of summer left. My friends and I have already come up with a money-making BUSINESS, taught a parrot how to RAP, invented a new kind of SLIME, taught a creeper how to FLY, and made a video go viral OVERNIGHT.

So, I'm just sayin' . . . who KNOWS what we'll think up next? This creeper can hardly wait to get started!!!

DON'T MISS ANY OF GERALD CREEPER JR.'S HILARIOUS ADVENTURES!

Sky Pony Press
New York